mary-kateandashley

TWO
of a **kind**™
Diaries

Look for these

titles:

mary-kateandashley

TWO of a kind™ Diaries

Winner Take All

by Lisa Banim

from the series created by
Robert Griffard & Howard Adler

HarperCollins*Entertainment*
An Imprint of HarperCollins*Publishers*

A PARACHUTE PRESS BOOK

A PARACHUTE PRESS BOOK
Parachute Publishing, L.L.C.
156 Fifth Avenue
Suite 325
NEW YORK
NY 10010
First published in the USA by Harper*Entertainment* 2000
First published in Great Britain by Collins 2002
HarperCollins*Entertainment* is an imprint of HarperCollins*Publishers* Ltd,
77-85 Fulham Palace Road, Hammersmith, London W6 8JB

1 3 5 7 9 8 6 4 2

ISBN 9780007144716

HarperCollins *Publishers*
1A Hamilton House, Connaught Place, New Delhi 110 001, India
77-85 Fulham Palace Road, London W6 8JB, United Kingdom
Hazelton Lanes, 55 Avenue Road, Suite 2900, Toronto, Ontario M5R 3L2
and 1995 Markham Road, Scarborough, Ontario M1B 5M8, Canada
25 Ryde Road, Pymble, Sydney, NSW 2073, Australia
31 View Road, Glenfield, Auckland 10, New Zealand
10 East 53rd Street, New York NY 10022, USA

Printed and bound at
Thomson Press (India) Ltd.

Chapter 1

Monday

Dear Diary,

Okay, okay! I admit it! I haven't written a single word to you in weeks. And I'm lying here on my bed feeling kind of guilty about it.

Dad wants me and my twin sister, Ashley, to keep track of absolutely everything that happens to us here at the White Oak Academy for Girls. But that's impossible!

Our dad and his research assistant, Carrie, are off hunting bugs in the Amazon right now. (Carrie also happens to be our fave babysitter!) The two of them are working on some big research project. It's going to last for five whole months. And that adds up to a lot of diary time.

But hey, it's not that I'm lazy – honest. You wouldn't believe all the stuff they keep us busy with here at boarding school. And that's not even counting homework.

1

Right now it's kind of hard to concentrate. That's because my roommate, Campbell Smith, is bouncing off the wall. Bouncing balls, that is. She does that a lot. I think it drives our next-door neighbours here in Porter House nuts. But I've got kind of used to it.

So anyway, Diary, it's almost a month since our Sadie Hawkins dance with the Harrington School for Boys. Ashley's been spending a lot of the time e-mailing her new boyfriend, Ross Lambert. It's tough to get any quality phone time around here (not to mention privacy!). And as for me, well . . .

What I have *not* been doing is spending time with a guy.

This morning Ashley met me in the dining hall for breakfast. She was wearing the fuzzy hot pink sweater Carrie gave her for Christmas and a long black skirt. "Wow," I said. "What's the big occasion?"

"Mary-Kate!" my sister said as she put down her tray at our usual table. "You know what day it is."

"Yeah," I said. "Monday."

"It's lab day. The day we share a class with the guys from Harrington," Ashley said. "Remember?"

Then she looked at me and frowned. "Judging from what you're wearing, I guess not."

I looked down at my White Oak sweatshirt and khaki pants. "What's the matter? I think I look okay."

Ashley sighed. "You do. It's just . . ."

"Just what?" I said.

My sister hesitated. "Look, Mary-Kate, I'll be blunt. If you want to get Grant Marino's attention, you've got to try a little harder. I mean, you guys really seemed to hit it off together at the dance. But he hasn't officially asked you out yet, right? And —"

"Uh, thanks, Ashley," I broke in. "I get your point."

"Sorry," Ashley said. "I was only trying to help. I'm sure things will work out for you and Grant. Eventually."

I stared into my lumpy oatmeal.

Ashley was right. Grant and I aren't exactly a couple like her and Ross. (If you count one Friday night movie together at the White Oak Performing Arts Centre as a relationship.)

I like Grant a lot. He's cute and super-nice. And we have tons in common – especially sports. Whenever I see him in class he always seems friendly. But that's the problem. He's *just* friendly.

I was going to change the subject. But I didn't have to. Dana Woletsky and her friend Kristin Lindquist walked by our table just then.

Dana is officially the most popular First Form (translation: seventh grade) girl at White Oak. She's pretty, I guess. She's got what Ashley calls "style". And she always has a zillion people around her. If you ask me, Dana's kind of snobby. But for some reason, Ashley is dying to hang out with her.

"Dana, hi!" Ashley called eagerly.

Dana tossed her perfectly layered, dark hair and gave my sister a nod. Then she turned back to Kristin.

Talk about rude. I don't think Dana has forgiven Ashley yet for stealing her boyfriend at the Sadie Hawkins dance. Even though Ross wasn't actually Dana's boyfriend in the first place. (Long story.)

Dana had her nose so high in the air that she didn't even see Hurricane Campbell heading her way. My roommate bumped straight into her with her tray.

"Whoops! Sorry, Dana," Campbell said cheerfully. "Hope I didn't spill any juice on you."

Dana just kind of frowned at her, then moved on.

"So, Mary-Kate," Campbell said, plunking herself down at our table. "All ready for the big try-outs tomorrow?"

"You bet," I said. Campbell's the pitcher for the Lower School softball team, the Mighty Oaks – the team I want to play for!

"Great," Campbell answered. She pushed a strand of her short brown hair back under her baseball cap and began to peel a banana.

Mrs. Prichard, the headmistress, was at our table in a flash. "Campbell," she said. "No hats in the dining hall, please." Then she hurried to help some poor First Former who'd knocked over a whole pitcher of OJ.

"Sorry, Mrs. P.," Campbell called after her. "I forgot."

She tossed her cap beside her tray and took a bite of her banana. "So, MK, Coach Salvatore's looking for a really strong hitter. You've got the stats, right?"

"Right," I said.

I hope so, anyhow. I've always been an ace hitter for my team back home in Chicago, the Belmont Bashers. I'm really excited about the try-outs for the Mighty Oaks tomorrow. But sort of nervous, too. What if I choke?

Ashley was staring at Campbell in amazement. Talk about choking. Campbell gulped down a big glass of milk, a granola bar, and three strips of bacon in about two seconds flat. "Breakfast of champions," Campbell said, with her mouth still full. "Gotta go. I want to get in a little practice before class." She jumped up, grabbed her tray and took off again.

"That girl sure does have a lot of energy," Ashley said.

"You should see her on the ball field," I said, watching Campbell bound out of the dining room.

Then I looked down at my bowl and thought about the big try-outs.

If Campbell and I were cereals, she would definitely be Wheaties.

What would I be?

Dear Diary,

It's almost midnight, and I'm writing this under the covers with a flashlight. (My roommate Phoebe gets super cranky if I wake her up.) Anyway, here goes:

Guess what? Ross asked me out again! Sort of. We only had a chance to talk for a couple of minutes after lab. We're going to the Dive (that's the Harrington Student Union) for burgers some Saturday night.

All I have to do is get Miss Viola's permission and I can take the shuttle bus over at six o'clock. They're awfully strict about dates here at White Oak. The teachers chaperone everyone and we have to be back in our rooms by nine-thirty sharp.

So how can I convince Mary-Kate to call Grant so the four of us can double?

I can tell Grant likes my sister. He always gives

her this big smile in lab. Maybe he's just shy about making the first move. I guess that means it's definitely up to Mary-Kate.

At any rate, tonight we had a popcorn party in the lounge downstairs. It was really fun. One of the best things about boarding school is that you get to be with your friends 24/7. That's pretty cool – most of the time, anyway.

And guess what, Diary? Dana showed up at the party. She lives in Phipps House next door, but she was visiting Kristin here in Porter.

The minute Dana arrived, everyone started crowding around her.

"Dana, I love your outfit," Lisa Dunmead said.

"When's your next party?" Lexy Martin said. "The last one was so awesome."

"What's going on at Harrington?" Fiona Ferris asked.

Dana made the rounds of the room. I just sat there beside Mary-Kate, stuffing my face with popcorn and feeling really left out.

If only Dana and I hadn't had that big misunderstanding about Ross. Then maybe the two of us could be friends and I'd be part of her superpopular group.

Don't get me wrong, Diary. I know I have new friends here at White Oak. And I'm having a great time. But listening to Dana tell all those funny stories about her party last week (which I definitely wasn't invited to) really burned me up.

Dana's not the only thing I have to worry about.

"Mary-Kate, you've got to sneak up to my room after lights-out," I whispered when the party was over. "I really need to talk to you."

Mary-Kate rolled her eyes. "Is this about Grant again? I'm telling you, I'm not going to ask him out."

I grabbed her by the arm. "It's not about Grant. I promise. But I really need your help."

Mary-Kate still looked a little suspicious. "Okay," she said finally. "If it's that important."

It was. I had to talk to my sister and Phoebe about my big interview tomorrow.

Diary, you know how much I've been dying to join the Lower School newspaper, the White Oak *Acorn*. Well, Ms. Bloomberg, my English teacher, is the faculty advisor. She's really tough. I don't know if she likes the way I write. I don't even know if she likes *me*. But if I want to work on the *Acorn*, I have to ask Ms. Bloomberg.

So I took a deep breath and walked up to her desk after class on Friday. Ms. Bloomberg was glancing through the essays we had just handed in.

Ms. Bloomberg peered at me over her glasses. "Yes, Ashley?"

"Um, I was wondering if I might be able to write for the *Acorn*," I said, talking really fast.

She looked at me for a long minute. "I must say, I was quite impressed with your essay on *The Diary of Anne Frank*," she said finally.

"Uh, thanks," I said, gulping.

"You had some original ideas, and your paper was very well written," Ms. Bloomberg went on. She paused and tapped a pencil on her desk. "Perhaps we *could* find a place for you on the *Acorn*."

"That'd be great," I said.

Ms. Bloomberg nodded. "Stop by the *Acorn* office on Tuesday afternoon," she said. "I'll set up a meeting for you with one of the Lower School editors. The final decision will be hers, of course."

"Gee, thanks, Ms. Bloomberg," I said, heading quickly towards the door.

"Oh, and Ashley!" my teacher called after me.

I turned around. Had Ms. Bloomberg changed her mind already?

"Three o'clock on Tuesday. Sharp."

I don't know why I'm so nervous about all this stuff, Diary. Maybe it's just because I'm in a new school, and it's so important for me to fit in. I really want to make a name for myself here at White Oak.

Anyway, after lights-out tonight, Mary-Kate and Phoebe sat on my bed and did their best to give me a pep talk.

"Ashley, you're a fantastic writer," Mary-Kate said. "Of course they'll put you on the paper. Tell her, Phoebe."

Phoebe pushed her blue-rimmed glasses farther up on her nose. I really do like my roommate, Diary. Even though we're pretty different. Like, Phoebe's into serious poetry and drama, and she has a whole closet full of funky vintage clothes. But she's a terrific friend. And she's totally – well – *sensible*.

"You showed me some of the stuff you wrote for your paper back home, Ashley," Phoebe said. "It was great." Then she stopped. "Wait a minute," she said. "We have plenty of room in the Poetry section."

Oops. How could I have forgotten that my own roommate was an editor for the *Acorn*? But *poetry*? Yikes!

"Gee, thanks, Phoebe," I said quickly. "But I'm not that good at making things rhyme."

"Oh. Well, let me know if you change your mind," Phoebe said.

We talked about other things for a while, like Mary-Kate's big softball try-out tomorrow. But as soon as Mary-Kate went back to her room and Phoebe started snoring, I began to get even more nervous about my meeting at the *Acorn*. I lay awake forever, trying to decide on the perfect outfit to wear.

Then I dreamed I had on one of those vintage polka-dot dresses from Phoebe's closet, along with a pair of – ugh – orthopaedic lace-up shoes.

It was such a bad nightmare that I woke up and couldn't go back to sleep. So that's why I'm writing to YOU, Diary!

Help!

chapter 2

Tuesday

Dear Diary,

It's lunchtime, and I came back to the dorm to change my hairstyle. I'm too jittery to eat, anyway.

I was so tired this morning that I almost fell asleep putting on my moisturiser. Phoebe kept asking me whether I was feeling okay.

"Sure," I said. "I'm just fine." Then I blinked the moisturiser right into my eyes.

I'd finally decided to go with the professional look: a cream-coloured turtleneck and my short checked skirt. But by now I was so nervous about meeting with the *Acorn* editor that I completely blanked on accessories.

Dressed for success

"Keep it simple," Phoebe advised. "My grandmother always says to put on three pieces of jewellery and take one off. That way, you won't overdo it."

12

"Do earrings count as two pieces or one?" I asked.

Phoebe shook her head. "Come on, Ashley. You're totally losing it here. You're not applying for a job at the *Chicago Tribune*, okay?" She threw up her hands. "I just don't understand why you're so worried, Ashley. Who *wouldn't* want you on the *Acorn* staff?"

"Thanks, Phoebe," I said. "Whatever they've got for me, I'm ready."

I *think*, I added to myself.

My big new confidence lasted all the way until English class. Ms. Bloomberg read an essay Dana had written about the theme of leadership in another book we were reading, *Lord of the Flies*.

Dana's essay was really good. When the bell rang at the end of the period, I went over to tell Dana what a great job she'd done. But she and Brooke Miller and Fiona Ferris were all whispering together. When the three of them saw me, they stopped talking. "Oh, hi, Ashley," Dana said. "See you later, okay?"

My mouth dropped open. See you *later*? Was that a total brush-off or *what*?

I hurried away so Dana and her friends wouldn't see how humiliated I was.

Why does that girl always make me feel like a fly?

13

Dear Diary,

Well, it's thirty minutes and counting until the try-outs. So I thought I'd come back to the room and write to you. Maybe it will help take my mind off things. Because I'm really in major trouble now. Here's what happened:

At lunch I looked everywhere for Ashley, but she wasn't around. Finally, I headed to the food line and loaded up on the speciality of the day: sloppy joes.

I sighed as I sat down at a table by myself. I have to tell you, Diary, I've been feeling a little homesick lately. I keep thinking about Dad and how he always tried to be there at all my games. Who was going to cheer for me today?

No one.

Also, I haven't had to try out for a team in ages. Everyone back home knows I'm a good player. I'm practically a Belmont Bashers legend. (Well, okay, maybe I'm exaggerating a little!) But things are probably way different here at the White Oak Academy for Girls.

I tried to snap myself out of it. So the Mighty Oaks aren't the Belmont Bashers, I told myself. The important thing is being part of a team.

"That's it!" I said aloud. I've always been a team player, right? And that was exactly what I needed to show Coach Salvatore today.

I snarfed down the rest of my sloppy joe and rushed out of the dining hall. Maybe I could help carry the equipment out to the field or something.

Then I saw Ashley heading towards me from the end of the hallway. "Mary-Kate, wait up!" she called, waving.

"Ashley, where were you?" I asked as she ran up. "You were supposed to meet me, remember?"

"Sorry," Ashley said breathlessly. "I lost track of time, I guess."

I frowned. "Wait a minute. Didn't you look different this morning?"

"I had to change my hair," Ashley said. "It was a mess."

"Aren't you going a little, uh . . . overboard with this whole interview thing?" I asked.

"Isn't that your lucky Belmont Bashers shirt?" Ashley shot back.

I sighed. "Okay, okay. I guess we're both pretty nervous. But we've got to keep a positive attitude. That's what Carrie's always telling us, right?"

Ashley nodded. "Right." Then she grinned and pretended to stick a microphone in front of my face. "Basher Burke," she said, in her best reporter voice. "Millions of fans want to know: will you lead your new team to victory today?"

I puffed myself up and chomped on a huge wad of imaginary gum like a major-league baseball player. "Well, that's a no-brainer, Ashley," I said. "The Mighty Oaks aren't bad, but they hit quite a slump last season. As you know, I am the greatest player ever. I'll whip those Oaks into shape and rule the ball field!"

Just then I happened to look over Ashley's shoulder. And guess who was standing there?

Coach Salvatore! And she'd heard the whole thing.

Boy, did I feel stupid. My face felt as hot as those nasty chili things Dad puts in his Knock 'Em Dead Nacho Casserole. Coach couldn't possibly think I was serious about the Oaks being losers, right?

She gave me a really funny look. "We'll see who's whipped into shape, Ms. Burke," she said. Then she marched away without another word.

Yikes. Time check, Diary.

Five minutes left on the clock. I guess I'm outta here.

Wish me luck!

chapter 3

Tuesday

Well, Diary,

Today was one of the most embarrassing days of my entire life. I totally blew the softball try-outs!

I have no clue what happened. I was trying so hard to make Coach Salvatore notice me. I just had to show her what a great team player I'd be for the Mighty Oaks.

Well, Coach noticed me, all right. Because I was the worst player on the field!

First, I blew an easy out at third. Then I dropped a fly ball. I grounded out at my first at bat and struck out four of the next five times. And in the fifth inning I was so eager to make a catch that I ran smack into another fielder.

Strike out!

17

Coach didn't say anything at all. She just kept making notes on her clipboard.

"Yo, MK, what's the matter?" Campbell asked. She jogged up as our team headed toward the dugout for the last inning.

"Beats me," I said with a sigh. "I'm having an off day, that's all."

Campbell looked back over her shoulder at Coach Salvatore. "Maybe you should explain that to Coach," she said. "You know, tell her you don't feel well or something."

"I feel fine," I said grumpily, choosing a new bat. But I couldn't help shivering a little. New Hampshire is freezing in late March. Even colder than Chicago.

Campbell hesitated. "Uh, Mary-Kate, about that team you played for at home – the Bashers? What kind of record did you guys have last season?"

That made me kind of mad. I mean, the Bashers are great! "We practically won the championship last year!" I said. "And I bet we – I mean they – *do* win it this year."

Only they'll have to win it without me. I keep forgetting. I'm not a Basher any more.

And if things kept going this way, I wasn't going to be an Oak, either.

Coach Salvatore tried all of us out in different positions. Except for Campbell, who was practically guaranteed the starting pitcher spot again. Every time I came to bat, Campbell gave me a thumbs-up. Then she pitched some wicked balls.

I tried my best, but I whiffed every time. Coach Salvatore just shook her head.

As Coach was making a final note on her clipboard, Campbell threw me one last pitch. A nice, easy one.

I shut my eyes and gave that swing everything I had.

Crack! I bet you could've heard the ball meet my bat all the way back in Chicago. Finally, I had a decent hit!

Well, okay, it wasn't *that* amazing. It was a grounder. But at least I got on base.

I looked back at Coach Salvatore. But I couldn't read her expression at all.

Would one lucky grounder be enough to land me a spot on the Oaks?

This would never have happened if I was playing for the Bashers.

Finally, the torture was over. Almost.

Coach Salvatore blew her whistle. "Okay, everybody!" she called. "Over here!"

All of the Oaks and wannabe Oaks gathered around as Coach announced the names of the kids who had made the first cut.

"Charlotte Atherton," Coach called out. "Kayla

Bailey. Mary-Kate Burke . . ."

I couldn't believe it! I still had a chance!

"Mary-Kate, you have definite potential," Coach said, taking me aside as we were leaving the field. "Think of this as a trial period. But you're really going to have to prove yourself if you want to make the second cut."

I promised I would try my best. "A trial period?" I whispered to Campbell back in the locker room. "That's the worst! Now every practice will feel like a try-out."

My roommate shrugged as she pulled her Mighty Oaks team sweatshirt over her head. "Don't worry," she said. "You'll be fine."

You know what, Diary? Maybe Campbell is right. If I want to make the Oaks, there's only one thing to do: P-R-A-C-T-I-S-E!

Mary-Kate Burke is no quitter. When the going gets tough, the tough get – hungry.

Guess it's time to head to dinner and hit the training table. Extra-protein tofu burgers, here I come!

(But first I'm going to send an e-mail to Max and Brian. Just to check up on what's new with the Bashers. I sure miss all of my old teammates. *Especially* today.)

Winner Take All

Dear Diary,

Well, I guess my interview at the Acorn went better than Mary-Kate's softball try-out. It was a little rough at first, though.

At three o'clock on the dot I walked into the staff room.

It's a pretty big office in the basement of the main building. There are framed awards and headlines on the walls, and rows of computers and layout tables, and even an old typewriter in the corner. There's paper everywhere, too, overflowing the recycling bins. What a mess. But it looks like a real working newspaper office.

I loved it.

An older girl with curly red hair and a pencil stuck behind her ear came up to me. "Hi, I'm Liz Sebastian. May I help you?" she asked.

"I'm Ashley Burke," I said, trying to sound extra confident. "I'm supposed to meet with one of the Lower School editors at three. Ms. Bloomberg sent me."

Liz nodded. "Oh, yeah. Right this way, Ashley."

Now, this is more like it, I told myself. I followed Liz to a tiny room in the back of the *Acorn* office.

"Good luck," Liz said. "See ya."

I peeked in to the office – and almost dived into one of those recycling bins.

Who was sitting behind the desk, but . . . Dana Woletsky!

She glanced up and gave me a really sour look.

"I was so *not* excited when Ms. Bloomberg told me I had to find a place for you on the staff," Dana said. "I'm the Special Features Editor. Have a seat."

Dana

There's no doubt about it, Diary. Dana is still mad at me for inviting Ross to the Sadie Hawkins dance. So why would she ask me to join the newspaper?

But I plopped down in a chair, anyway. Dana checked stuff on the computer and made a couple of phone calls. I sat and twiddled my thumbs.

Finally, Dana put down the phone and looked at me. "Sorry," she said. "There's just so much to do here on the paper. I'm sure you understand."

"Absolutely," I agreed quickly. "I know all about being on a newspaper staff. When I was at my old school in Chicago—"

"So when Ms. Bloomberg called about you yesterday," Dana interrupted me, "I had to tell her, we do need another writer." She leaned forward over her desk. "I have a job for you if you want it."

"You do?" I was so excited, my voice squeaked. "Doing what?"

"I think you'd be perfect as—" Dana paused dramatically – "the new First Form gossip columnist."

A gossip columnist? I was so surprised, I didn't know what to think. Gossip columnists had to find out stuff nobody wanted them to know. That could be fun.

Or it could get me into trouble.

On the other hand, being a gossip columnist would be a perfect way for me to find out what was really going on at White Oak. I'd get the scoop on what was in, what was out – and all the best parties!

And it might give me an in with Dana and her whole crowd. They knew everyone and everything at White Oak – and Harrington, too.

I was starting to like this idea.

"Well, what do you say?" Dana asked.

I took a deep breath. "Okay," I said. "I'll do it."

"Great," she said. "Look, you'll have tons of freedom. You can write about *whatever* you want – as long as it's new and different."

"Great," I said. This was sounding better and better. First I'd need a cool name for my column. Next to my picture, of course . . .

Then Dana dropped the bombshell. "We'll expect a column for the next issue," she said. "The *Acorn* comes out every Saturday. That means you have to turn your story in on Wednesday."

I gulped. That meant my first deadline was – *tomorrow*?

"And if you don't get this column in on time, I won't be able to put it in until next week," Dana warned. "By that time any hot gossip will be old news. Do you have a problem with that?"

"No problem at all," I told her.

Dana raised her eyebrows. "Okay," she said. "I'll tell the layout people to leave the space open."

I got up to leave. "Thanks so much for this terrific opportunity, Dana. You won't be sorry."

Dana flipped her supershiny dark hair. "I sure hope not," she said. "Good luck."

I left the *Acorn* office and headed straight to the main Student Lounge upstairs. What better place to start scooping out material for my column?

And who knows, Diary? If I can impress Dana with a great story, we might even end up being friends after all!

chapter 4

Tuesday

Dear Diary,

Campbell and I are taking a study break right now. We started off with a little throwing and catching practice here in our room. "You know, I'm still worried about making the team," I said, pitching from my bed. "I don't think Coach Salvatore likes me much."

Campbell went to retrieve the ball. "Coach is tough, but she's fair," she said from behind the desk. "If you try hard and play well, she'll like you. No problem."

I wound up and threw the ball back – just as the door opened.

"Hey, watch out!" Ashley ducked as the ball whizzed by her head. "You'll hurt someone."

She flopped down on my bed.

"Listen, I really need your help. I eavesdropped on practically every conversation at dinner. And talked to tons of people in the student lounge. And snooped outside every room on the floor. I'm totally *desperate!*"

Huh? Campbell and I just stared at her. Sometimes Ashley gets a little overdramatic. "Are you by any chance referring to your new column for the paper?" I said finally.

"Of *course* that's what I'm talking about!" Ashley threw up her hands. "How am I ever going to come up with a major story overnight? It's impossible!"

The three of us thought for a minute.

"Hey," Campbell said, "I've got an idea for you."

My sister brightened. "Really? What? Tell me quick!"

"Well, this girl on our team, Ellen, has athlete's foot," Campbell offered.

I groaned. Campbell was totally serious!

Ashley looked a little alarmed. "Um . . . thanks, Campbell," she said politely.

Then she bounced off the bed and out of our room as fast as she'd blown in.

Today sure has been one for the record books. Whose was worse, mine or Ashley's?

Dear Diary,

(8:00 P.M.) Help! I still haven't written one single word on my computer.

This whole gossip column thing is going to be a bust. How can I possibly come up with enough decent material by tomorrow? And why did I ever tell Dana I could do it?

(8:10) I keep racking my brains, but . . . nothing.

(8:20) Double nothing.

(8:30) Triple nothing.

(8:35) STILL NOTHING!!! I am toast. Burned toast.

Dear Diary,

It's me again. I'm sure you'll be happy to hear that I finally have my story! Here's how it happened:

"There's no way I can concentrate," I told Phoebe, pushing back my chair at eight forty-five. "I need a snack. Preferably of the junk-food variety."

Phoebe looked up from her history book. "Maybe you shouldn't have skipped the make-your-own-sundae bar at dinner," she said. "You could check in the dining hall and see if there's anything left."

I sighed. "It's probably an ice-cream-soup bar by now. I guess I'm stuck with something from the vending machines downstairs." I headed for the door.

"Get me a pack of peanuts, okay?" Phoebe called after me.

I ran down the stairs and tried to tiptoe past our housemother's room. We're really not supposed to leave our floor during study hours.

But as I got to the bottom step, I stopped. Miss Viola's door was open – and she was playing her stereo. Not nice, quiet classical music, either. It was loud and it was country! I could definitely hear a banjo.

I knocked, but Miss Viola didn't hear me. She had her back turned to me. And she was *line dancing*!

I think.

It was hard to tell, because Miss Viola's moves looked pretty weird. She was using one of those videotapes that shows you how to do the steps. And she was really terrible.

I couldn't wait to get back upstairs and tell everyone Miss Viola likes to line dance.

Then I had an absolutely brilliant idea. "Yes!" I cried, jumping up and punching the air.

I instantly forgot about that crunchy chocolate snack I'd been craving. This was just the story I needed for my column!

I raced back to my room and whipped off a quick

first draft. It was so easy. The words just seemed to write themselves.

Then I felt someone looking over my shoulder. It was Phoebe.

"Gosh, Ash," she said, shaking her dark curly hair. "Don't you think that's a little . . . much?"

"What do you mean?" I asked, frowning. "I think it's pretty good."

"Well, it is," Phoebe said slowly. "But you have to be careful. Maybe you should make your column funnier. More lighthearted. You don't want to hurt Miss Viola's feelings, right? And hey, lots of people like country music."

I looked at my story again. Phoebe was right. It did need more humour. And maybe I should take out that part about the injured cow.

So I revised my article a bit – you know, exaggerated the funny stuff a little. Then I printed out my new version and handed it to Phoebe.

She nodded her approval. My first gossip column for the White Oak *Acorn* was officially done!

But as I clicked the "send" command on my e-mail, I had a teensy feeling of doubt.

Would Dana like my first column?

And what about – Miss Viola?

chapter 5

Saturday

Dear Diary,

Just a quick note for now – I'm only stopping by the room to get my mitt. I need to put in some major practice time after lunch.

I sure do love Saturdays.

While I'm here, I might as well check my computer. Excellent! I have mail! Later, Diary . . .

Okay, I'm back. But I only have a sec.

The first e-mail was from Dad. He and Carrie are having a great time in the Amazon. They're finding lots of bugs and spiders, too. (Remind me to stay away from bird-eating tarantulas. They're eleven inches long – and *super*hairy!) Their research project is turning out to be a big success.

It makes me sort of dizzy to think of Dad and Carrie so far away

Super spider!

in a jungle somewhere. But hey, what's five months? By now there are only two months, two weeks, and one day left till the end of the term at White Oak.

Not that I'm counting or anything, Diary. I love it here at boarding school, I really do. And I've got plenty of things to look forward to. Like playing for the Mighty Oaks.

I hope.

The second e-mail was from Max! I taped it in.

Hi, Mary-Kate, how are you? We're okay but we got creamed in our first game against the Hawks yesterday. 8-ZIP. We need a decent hitter fast or the championships are history this season. Marty Lopez took your place at third. But he stinks at bat. Good luck with your new team. Don't forget your old Basher buddies, okay? See ya, Max P. S. WRITE BACK.

I read the note again. Max's spelling sure has improved. Or maybe he used the spell checker on his computer.

Why are my eyes itching like this? I have to let them water up a little to make it stop. I am *not* crying, Diary. I'm a Basher, remember?

Dear Diary,

Lunch was a little more eventful than usual today.

When Mary-Kate met me at our usual table in the dining hall, her eyes looked kind of puffy.

"Hey, what's wrong?" I asked. "Is everything okay? Did you flunk a test or something? Did Coach Salvatore kick you off the team?"

"Nothing's wrong," Mary-Kate said. But she had that grumbly voice that means leave-me-alone-I-don't-want-to-talk-about-it-right-now. I can read my sister like a book.

"But you've been crying," I said, frowning. "Come on, Mary-Kate, spill it."

I thought Mary-Kate was going to throw her tray of baked ziti at me. "Look," she said. "I don't want to talk about it, okay? To tell you the truth, I'd rather just be left alone for a little while."

See what I mean?

I shut up.

Luckily, a whole bunch of people came to sit with us: Phoebe, Alyssa Fuji, Wendy Linden, and Wendy's roommate, Jolene Dupree. Jolene's from Alabama, and she has this amazing Southern drawl.

"Hi guys!" I said brightly. I was kind of relieved to have some company right then. Mary-Kate wasn't exactly being chatty.

But boy, was she hungry.

"Hey, Mary-Kate, what's up with all the pasta?" Wendy asked. Mary-Kate had just returned with a second plate of ziti, garlic bread, and a side bowl of macaroni and cheese. Yuck.

"I'm carbo-loading," Mary-Kate explained. "All this starchy stuff will turn to sugar later and give me lots of energy for practice this afternoon. Campbell says it really helps."

Phoebe raised her eyebrows. "What about all the cheese and garlic butter and tomato sauce?"

Carbed-out

"The carbohydrates are underneath," Mary-Kate said, shrugging. "In the bread and pasta. That's what counts."

"Well, if you eat any more pasta, you'll explode," I told her.

Mary-Kate just glared at me. Oops.

Saved again! Just then the heavy oak doors to the dining hall opened and Dana Woletsky walked in. Kristin Lindquist and Ms. Bloomberg were with her. Each of the girls was carrying a box. The latest issue of the White Oak *Acorn* had arrived!

Ms. Bloomberg started calling tables up a few at a time to get papers.

I couldn't wait to see my column in print. But I was a little nervous, too. Phoebe and Mary-Kate both jumped up and grabbed a whole bunch of papers for our table.

I flipped quickly through my copy. There it was, on page three: "The First Form Buzz" by Ashley Burke. And next to the column was my picture! It was a little blurry – I had to use my last year's yearbook photo on such short notice. But overall I thought the whole thing looked great.

I held my breath. What would everyone else think?

"Try to imagine an elephant at a hoedown," Phoebe read aloud, "and you'll get the idea. Our very own Porter House housemother isn't heavy or anything, but—"

"What's a hoedown?" Mary-Kate interrupted.

"Shh," Wendy told her, frowning.

"When Miss Viola hits the dance floor, you should, too – ace first, for cover!" Phoebe kept reading.

Everyone at the table started cracking up.

Phew! My column was a hit!

"Just make sure you don't get stepped on," Phoebe continued. "But with Miss Viola's fancy footwork, that may be impossible!"

Jolene picked up on the next part. "We can't wait till next year's Sadie Hawkins dance," she read. "Maybe Miss Viola will show us all how to do-si-do like pros. Pro wrestlers, that is."

At that, Jolene and Alyssa got up and began to swing each other around as if they were square dancing.

Some girls behind us began to snicker and clap their hands. "Oooh, Miss Viola, will you dance with me?" one of them called to Jolene.

"I think I'm going to sit this one out," a voice said.

Everyone froze. Mary-Kate even stopped eating.

It was Miss Viola!

I tried to slip lower in my seat. I wanted to totally disappear. Like, straight through the floor.

"Uh-oh," I heard Mary-Kate say under her breath.

How did Miss Viola like my article? I had a feeling I knew the answer to that one.

"H-hi, Miss Viola," I stammered. "Did you, um, see my column?"

Our housemother just nodded.

"It was supposed to be funny," I rushed on. "You shouldn't take it seriously or anything." I glanced at Miss Viola out of the corner of my eye. I couldn't read her expression at all.

No one at the table said a word.

Then Miss Viola actually *smiled* at me! "That was a very amusing article, Ashley," she said. "I always appreciate a good sense of humour."

I breathed a huge sigh of relief.

"But from now on, I'll be sure to close my door

when I'm pounding around like an elephant." Miss Viola smiled again – kind of – and started back across the dining room.

A lot of girls giggled as she walked by.

Miss Viola wasn't mad! So I guess I'm on the right track with this gossip column thing! Dana even gave me a thumbs-up on our way out of the dining hall.

There's just one problem. Now I'm going to have to come up with something even better for next week's column! And Wednesday isn't that far away . . .

chapter 6

Tuesday

Dear Diary,

Here I am, flopped on my bed again. But this time I have a hot water bottle for my upset stomach, thanks to that nice nurse in the infirmary.

Campbell is doing sit-ups. I counted for her for a while, but then I had to give up.

She's in great shape. I'm not. And practice this afternoon was a BTW: Big-Time Washout.

Coach Salvatore started us off running sprints. Easy, I thought. I was all revved up to show her what great shape I'm in.

I started off at the front of the pack. But my legs felt like they were filled with lead. Or maybe it was spaghetti and creamed corn, the carbo lunch specials of the day.

"Let's move it, guys!" Coach

Spaghetti legs

Salvatore called. "Pick up the pace, Burke!"

Two minutes later, the others were starting to leave me in the dust. (Actually, it's slush right now.)

What was I thinking when I ate that last bowl of corn? I groaned to myself, panting. I don't even like the stuff.

My stomach hurt so much that I could only make it through the first group of sprints. Then I had to sit down.

"Pacing, Mary-Kate, pacing!" Coach Salvatore said again, coming up to the bench. "Maybe we need to work a bit on our conditioning. More time spent on the indoor track in the field house might work wonders."

"No problem, Coach," Campbell said, jogging up. "I'll take Mary-Kate to the gym with me every morning before breakfast."

Breakfast, I thought, feeling even more nauseous. Ugh. The famous White Oak Oatmeal. Carb City.

Campbell peered at me more closely. "Hey, MK, are you okay?" she asked.

"Just ducky," I said, clutching my stomach again.

Coach Salvatore frowned. "Mary-Kate, I think you've had enough practice for today. I want you to stop by the nurse on your way back to your dorm."

"Nurse?" I said in alarm. "I'm fine, Coach, really I am. I just ate too much at lunch, that's all."

Coach didn't look convinced. "Better pack it in, Burke," she said. "Maybe you'll feel better tomorrow."

So that was it. I'd been kicked out of practice. And I'd probably be kicked off the team soon, too.

Well, Diary, at least there's a bright side to this stupid softball slump. Between worrying about Coach Salvatore and doing endless schoolwork, I have zippo time to think about Grant.

He still hasn't called me.

I guess he's never going to. But I was pretty sure he liked me. Why do guys do this kind of stuff?

It's driving me crazy.

Dear Diary,

I don't know how much time I have to write before Lisa and Lexy get back from dinner. (I'll explain later.) But I've got lots to tell you, so I'll start, anyway.

This afternoon around four I called Ross in his dorm at Harrington – and I actually got through! We talked for so long (I am seriously low on laundry quarters now) that the two girls waiting behind me ganged up and tried to strangle me with the phone cord.

Just kidding. But I did have to apologise to them. A lot.

Ross was so sweet, Diary. He was trying to help me think of an idea for my next column. Remember I told you I was going to come up with something better this time? Well, so far I've got . . . nada. Tomorrow is Wednesday – my deadline to Dana – and I'm totally scoopless.

Speaking of Dana, guess who came by just as I was hanging up?

"Well, hi, Ashley," Dana said. She looked totally cool in her black velour off-the-shoulder top and great-fitting jeans. "I'm on my way to Kristin's room for an ice-cream and makeover party. What are you up to right now?"

I stood up straighter. Was Dana actually going to invite me to the party? I was about to answer, but Dana beat me to it.

"Oh, that's right!" she said, with a wave of her perfectly-manicured hand. "How could I forget? Your column's due tomorrow. Is it finished yet?"

I gulped. "Um, not exactly."

Dana looked very sympathetic. "Don't worry, Ashley," she said. "I'm sure you'll think of something terrific. After all, your last column was so awesome. *Everyone* was talking about it last week."

"Thanks," I said, staring down at the floral carpet. Why couldn't I think of something else to say? I'm usually not at a loss for words. (In case you haven't noticed, Diary.)

"Well, happy writing," Dana said, turning away. She waggled those long red nails at me again. "Like I said, deadlines are very important at the *Acorn*. But don't let the pressure get to you or anything."

I gritted my teeth and smiled. "No problem, Dana."

But it *was* a problem. A big one.

Suddenly, Dana turned around *Dead line* on her way down the hall. "Oh, Ashley," she said. "I have a suggestion for you. Why don't you write about a student this time? And if I were you, I'd definitely make this column a little . . . edgier."

I wasn't sure what Dana meant by that.

"You know, make it juicier," Dana explained breezily. "And e-mail it to me the minute you're done, okay? See ya."

Yikes. I thought my Miss Viola story was already on the edge. But I really do want to impress Dana.

I sighed. While Dana and her buds were doing each other's hair, I'd be tearing my hair *out* trying to come up with a juicy story.

I had almost reached my room when I happened to notice that my next-door neighbours' door was open. I went in to grill Lisa and Lexy for Buzz ideas, but they weren't around. They were probably still at dinner.

While I was in their room, I kind of wandered around a bit. You know, just while I was waiting for them to get back. And guess what I saw peeking out from behind the bulletin board above Lexy Martin's desk?

A pair of crusty old sweat socks in a plastic sandwich bag!

That's weird, I thought. Extremely weird.

I looked closer. Then I pulled on the bag a little – and something small and white fluttered to the floor.

I picked it up. It was a scrap of notebook paper. And on it someone had written "My Lucky Socks!!!!!"

Hmmm. Talk about dirty laundry. Is there something here for my column?

I definitely need to get the four-one-one on *this*.

Whoops, I've got to go, Diary – I think I just heard someone go into Lexy and Lisa's room.

Over and out!

P. U.!

chapter 7

Thursday

Dear Diary,

It's Thursday already – and I never finished telling you the Lexy sock story! I've been kind of busy, though.

After I finally wrote my column Tuesday night (I'm getting to that part!), I had tons of schoolwork to catch up on. Right now I'm in the library, trying to plough through *A Light in the Forest*. But I keep falling asleep. I sure do need to catch some zzzzzs!

Being a staff writer for the *Acorn* is hard work. It takes up a lot of your time – not to mention your social life. (Sorry, Ross!) But it's definitely worth it.

People keep coming up to tell me how funny my first column was. And everyone wants to find out what – and who – my next story's about. But Dana's the only person who knows.

We're going to keep it a secret until the *Acorn* comes out on Saturday.

So okay, Diary. Here's what happened Tuesday night:

It wasn't superhard to get the scoop on those gross socks of Lexy's. When I went next door again, Lisa Dunmead was there. She hadn't been hanging out in the dining hall like I thought. She'd been in the shower. She was wearing a cute terry bathrobe with pink teapots on it and fuzzy pink slippers.

"So, Lisa," I said casually, "I was just wondering. What's the story on those old socks behind Lexy's bulletin board?"

Lisa looked a little startled. Then she tightened the towel turban around her long black curls. "Well, actually, Lexy doesn't like to talk about them much," she said.

"Why not?" I asked.

Lisa shrugged. "Bad luck, I guess," she said.

Now I was totally confused. "Bad luck?"

Lisa leaned closer and lowered her voice. "You know Lexy plays basketball, right?"

I nodded. Like, duh. *Everyone* knows that. Lexy

Martin is only the best First Form b-ball player at White Oak. Even better than some of the varsity players. It probably helps that she's about six feet tall already.

So far, this wasn't much of a scoop.

"Well, anyway," Lisa went on, "Those are Lexy's lucky socks."

Right. That's what the note said.

"She wears them to every single game," Lisa continued. "And guess what?"

"Gee, what?" I said. I was really trying to dig up a little enthusiasm now.

"She never *ever* washes them!" Lisa finished gleefully.

Hmmm, I thought. Now we're getting somewhere!

"White Oak hasn't lost a single game since Lexy started wearing those socks," Lisa explained. "So now she thinks she has to wear them!"

"Don't they stink up the room?" I asked, wrinkling my nose. Just the thought made me want to gag!

"They used to," Lisa admitted. "In fact, I almost asked Mrs. Prichard for a new roommate. But then Lexy put them in a plastic bag, so I don't notice the smell so much any more."

My fingers started itching. I couldn't wait to get back to my room and start that article!

"And here's the funniest part." Lisa looked towards the door, checking to make sure Lexy wasn't coming.

"Those socks used to belong to Lexy's brother," she rushed on. "He was a big player for Harrington a couple of years ago. I guess they were his lucky socks, too. Isn't that weird?"

Bingo!

I didn't actually tell Lisa that I was planning to use all the stuff she was telling me for my column. But I was sure Lexy wouldn't mind. After all, she was wearing those socks for the good of her team, right?

B-ball socks

Sorry, Diary, but I've got to get out of the library. It's way too quiet and I'm falling asleep!

Dear Diary,

Help!

I'm lying on the floor in my room, and I'm never getting up again.

I can't move a single muscle. Even for dinner. Campbell left half an hour ago. If I'm lucky, maybe she'll bring me back some quality carbs from the dining hall. As in cookies.

MARY-KATE'S DIARY

We've been getting up early every morning to run. Then we go to the weight room. After team practice, we stay after everyone else leaves. Campbell pitches, I hit. Over and over and over again. I do fine when Coach isn't watching.

"I don't get it," Campbell keeps saying, shaking her head.

I don't get it, either.

I was going to write to Max to ask his advice. But I just can't do it, Diary. It's way too embarrassing. How can I tell Max I can't hit under pressure any more?

Besides, it sounds as if he and the rest of the Bashers are having problems of their own. They lost two more games! Ouch. Max says the whole team wants me back.

Sometimes I really wish I could go.

So anyway, Diary, here's what else is going on. It's the weirdest thing, but I haven't seen much of Ashley lately. I went by her room the other night, but she was working on her stupid column again. She said she was too busy to talk – HA!

She's like, obsessed with getting new scoops for her column. She's always asking people questions and making notes on this little notepad she carries in her knapsack.

But what really makes me mad is the way Ashley's trying to get in with Dana Woletsky and her snobby friends. At lunch today they even came by our table to eat with Ashley and completely ignored me.

It's so obvious, it's embarrassing. Ashley spent lunch *whispering* something about her new article in Dana's ear! Like it was some big secret.

Dana shook her head. "Wow. That's amazing, Ashley. Where do you find this stuff, anyway?" she said.

"I bet it's something pretty hysterical," Summer Sorensen added. Summer's another one of the Dana clones. Except she looks like one of those blonde California surfer girls. She has a tan even in the winter.

"So what is your column going to be about this time?" I asked Ashley. I spooned up the last of the peppermint-stick ice cream we were sharing.

Ashley smiled at Dana. "You'll just have to wait and see like everybody else," she told me mysteriously.

That really made me mad. *Everybody else*? Who does Ashley think she is? I know who I am: her twin sister!

Then Dana and Summer left, and Ashley changed the subject. "So, Mary-Kate," she said casually. "What's going on with Grant? Have you heard from him at all?"

I sighed. Ashley knows perfectly well how

things are going on the guy front. They aren't. Period.

"Promise me you'll talk to him next time you see him," Ashley said. "I'll go with you if you want. You know, to break the ice."

"Thanks," I said. "But I don't think so."

It's not that I'm afraid to talk to Grant. He's totally nice to me in class and all, but that's about it.

Maybe he just thinks of me as a sports buddy or something. Wait till he finds out I'm probably not going to be on the Mighty Oaks much longer. He'll think I'm a loser for sure.

This romance stuff is tough. And to tell you the truth, I'm not sure I feel like talking about my love life (correction: nonlove life) with Ashley right now.

So where is Carrie when I need to ask her advice? In the Amazon, for Pete's sake.

"Promise me, Mary-Kate," Ashley was saying again.

"Okay, okay," I told her. "I'll talk to Grant."

But I made sure to cross my fingers.

chapter 8

Saturday

Dear Diary,

The *Acorn* came out today! Everyone in the student lounge is talking about it right now. I'm having a hard time writing this because it's so noisy. And people keep coming up to congratulate me.

My Lexy-socks story is a big success!

With *most* people, anyway. I don't see Lexy or Lisa or Phoebe or Mary-Kate or any of the girls from the basketball team in here. I guess they have other stuff to do. Even though everyone from both Porter and Phipps always hangs out here in the lounge after lunch on Saturdays.

All through lunch Phoebe was telling me and Wendy and Mary-Kate about some drama club thing. But it was hard for me to concentrate. I kept looking toward the dining-hall doors. It seemed like it was taking forever for the new issues to arrive.

To tell you the truth, I was getting that teeny nervous feeling again. Okay, the *way* nervous feeling. Kind of like the one I got after writing that article about Miss Viola.

Except it was worse this time.

Even though we're next-door neighbours, I don't know Lexy Martin too well. She isn't around that much, except for our weekly pizza parties and stuff. Most of her friends are on the basketball team and they live in Phipps House next door.

Anyway, Ms. Bloomberg and Dana finally showed up with the *Acorn* boxes. "Come and get them, people!" Ms. Bloomberg called. "One table at a time, please."

While I was waiting, I craned my neck, looking for Lexy.

She wasn't too hard to spot. For one thing, like I said before, she's pretty tall. And she also has this long, wavy, bright red hair.

Lexy was sitting at a table all by herself, wearing her basketball uniform. She was eating a bowl of soup and reading a book. It didn't seem like she was in a big hurry to get a paper.

Should I go over and say something to her now? I wondered. To warn her, maybe?

51

But before I could get up, Dana breezed over to Lexy's table and dropped an *Acorn* right under her nose. "Enjoy," I heard her say.

I frowned. Now why did Dana do that?

By this time everyone at my table was reading the paper. Mary-Kate turned straight to the Buzz.

"So this is it?" she said, after a minute. "The big secret?"

I nodded. "What do you think?" I asked.

Phoebe cleared her throat. "Well, the story's pretty funny," she said. "I guess."

"I think it's even better than your Miss Viola article," Wendy said.

But Mary-Kate snorted and tossed her paper on to her lunch tray. "Give me a break. 'Generations of lucky bugs live in a secret pair of tube socks handed down in a certain White Oak/Harrington family b-ball dynasty'? What is this, a TV soap opera? If you want my opinion, Ashley, it's kind of stupid."

Lucky bugs

Stupid? I was shocked. "What's *that* supposed to mean?" I demanded.

Just then, a bunch of girls giggled at the table beside us. I turned around. Samantha Clark was nodding towards Lexy, grinning and holding her nose.

Luckily, Lexy didn't notice. She was busy reading

the *Acorn*. Page three.

"Hey, congratulations, Ashley," Mary-Kate said. "Dana seems really happy with your article."

I looked across the dining hall. You're not going to believe this, Diary – Dana was actually waving me over! I was going to get to sit at the cool table for the rest of lunch!

"Excuse me," I told everyone, picking up my tray. "I'll see you later, okay?"

"Have fun," Phoebe muttered.

On the way to Dana's table, I had to pass Lexy Martin. But she wasn't alone any more. A whole bunch of girls wearing White Oak basketball uniforms had gone through the lunch line and come to sit with her.

Lexy didn't even glance at me as I walked by. I've got to say something, I told myself. But the truth was, I couldn't seem to face my next-door neighbour at all.

Lexy was talking and laughing with her friends as if nothing had happened. But I couldn't help noticing that Lexy's usually pale skin was hot pink under her freckles. I didn't catch what she was saying since I walked by so fast, but her voice seemed extra high.

A major stab of guilt ran through me. You know what, Diary? I hate to admit it, but maybe Mary-Kate was right.

Maybe that article about Lexy and her stinky socks was stupid.

Really stupid.

But wait a minute, Diary. Isn't everyone telling me how funny my column was? Didn't I sit at the cool table at lunch? And Lexy seemed perfectly fine when she left the dining hall with her friends, right?

Maybe I'm making too big a deal out of this whole thing.

The stinky socks story was *great*.

Dear Diary,

I was just leaving my room this afternoon when Ashley jumped out at me from the hallway.

"Are you going somewhere?" Ashley asked.

I showed her my mitt and gym bag. "Campbell's waiting for me down at the field house," I said.

"Well, I really need to talk to you," Ashley said. "Please, Mary-Kate."

I started to walk past her. "And to what do I owe this honour?" I asked. I know that sounded snooty, but I couldn't help it. I'm still kind of mad about the way she's been treating me lately.

At first Ashley looked hurt. Then she frowned. "Quit it, Mary-Kate," she said. "This is important."

I hoisted my bag on to my shoulder. "Okay, what?"

Ashley sighed. "Well, I just came back to the dorm to get my lab notes for that test we have next week. And when I went by Lisa and Lexy's room, those grotty lucky socks were sticking out of Lexy's trash basket! Do you know what that means?"

"Yeah," I said. "It means that White Oak's going to start losing all their basketball games. And it's all your fault."

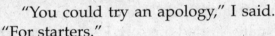

Ashley rolled her eyes. "It *means* that maybe I hurt Lexy's feelings after all. What should I do?"

"You could try an apology," I said. "For starters."

"I already did that," Ashley said, slumping against the wall. "Lexy said it was no problem, that the socks were just a joke, anyway. But she had these funny pink spots on her cheeks."

"Can you blame her?" I asked.

"Well, next time I'm going to write about something completely different," Ashley said. "I'll just have to come up with an idea on my own."

I looked at my watch. By now I was really late. Campbell had probably logged ten miles on the indoor track already.

"Listen, Ashley, I'm really sorry," I said. "But I have to go. We'll talk later, okay?"

"Okay," Ashley said with a sigh.

I started down the stairs, then turned around. "Hey, Coach called a special practice this afternoon at five. I think she's getting pretty close to making a decision about final cuts. Can you come down to the field and sort of cheer me on?"

"Sure, Mary-Kate," Ashley said. "I wouldn't miss it."

"Thanks," I said, bounding down the stairs. "Remember, the softball field. Five o'clock. Moral support."

Ashley leaned over the banister and grinned. "I'll be there," she said. "Twin's promise."

But you know what, Diary? She never showed up.

Practice actually started off okay. I even managed a few hits. But I was so busy looking for my sister that I missed an easy fly ball. And after that it was all downhill.

"Come on, MK," Campbell called as I hit a third foul off the fence behind me. "You can do it!"

I choked up on the bat. That's what Ashley should be saying, I thought.

"Strike one!" called Cassie Brunelli, the Third Form girl who was acting as umpire.

Whiff!

"Strike two!" Cassie shouted.

Playing downhill

I wanted to bash the ball to pieces. But I swung and missed again.

"Strike three!" Cassie said, pointing me out.

Game over.

"Okay, hit the showers, everyone!" Coach called. "Mary-Kate, maybe you should put in a few rounds on the ball machine."

I threw my bat on the ground. Twin's promise, I thought. Ha!

On my way back from the field – alone – I saw Ashley hanging outside the Student Union with Dana and Kristin. They seemed to be having a big laugh over something. Probably me.

I can't believe my sister blew me off like that!

chapter 9

Sunday

Dear Diary,

Well, here I am, all alone in my room on a rainy Sunday afternoon with nothing but a fruit roll-up for company. And I'm getting a little sick of staring out the window through Phoebe's bead curtains.

I guess all good journalists have to worry about finding the perfect story for their columns. Then they have to stress over getting all the right info.

So what am I going to write about next? You know, Diary, my brain never used to freeze up like this when I wrote for our school paper back in Chicago.

And this time I'm definitely on my own. Mary-Kate seems a little mad at me. Probably because I missed her softball practice yesterday.

That was a mistake. But I didn't mean to, Diary. Honest. I was on my way down to the field when I ran into Dana. And I guess we got a little caught up.

Phoebe hasn't been much help, either. She's off at the Performing Arts Centre right now, at a drama club meeting. She's been hanging around the theatre a lot lately. Probably because the drama club's going to put on a play with Harrington. It's

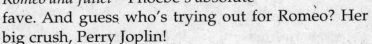

Romeo and Juliet – Phoebe's absolute fave. And guess who's trying out for Romeo? Her big crush, Perry Joplin!

Since I can't seem to come up with any brilliant ideas, I just e-mailed Dad to ask whether he got the first Buzz article I sent him. I got a letter from him today, but he didn't mention it.

I'm thinking maybe I should try out the purple lip gloss on Phoebe's dresser. I'm sure she won't mind. It's not exactly my colour, but still . . .

Whoops, Diary, I've got to go! Someone's at the door.

Dear Diary,
  Okay, I'm back! It's almost time for dinner, but if I write fast I think I can tell you everything.

You'll never guess who it was at the door. Dana! She was all dressed up in this amazing black skirt and sweater and cute high boots. Her parents came and took her out to brunch at Le Château today. Dana is *so* sophisticated!

"Hi, Ashley," Dana said. "How about grabbing some hot chocolate or something with me downstairs?"

I quickly tried to smudge off the last of that gross purple lip stuff. "Sure," I said. "Sounds great."

For some reason, I felt kind of funny walking downstairs beside Dana. Some girls who were waiting for the pay phone in the hall turned around and looked at me.

I guess this means I'm officially popular now. I mean, Dana doesn't even live in our dorm. Kristin has a single room at the end of my hall, but she didn't seem to be around anywhere.

Did Dana come just to see *me*?

The Porter House lounge was pretty empty, for once. This afternoon there were just a couple of girls playing handheld computer games in the corner.

"So, Ashley," Dana said, handing me a packet of cocoa mix from the counter and heating up a pot of water on the hot plate. "How are things going with you and Ross?"

Uh-oh, I thought, gulping. Here it comes.

"Um, fine," I answered. "He's a really sweet guy."

"He sure is," Dana said. She poured out some boiling water into a mug and added instant cocoa.

"You and Ross make such a cute couple," Dana went on. "Do you want marshmallows or whipped cream?"

Dana sure was being understanding about the whole Ross situation. And I thought she'd be mad at me forever! What a relief.

Dana and I settled in on one of the couches with our hot drinks. Then Dana got right down to business.

"So, is your column finished yet, Ashley?" she asked.

I should have known. This wasn't a social call.

"Not yet," I said. "But I'm definitely working on it."

Dana nodded. "Well, I've been thinking that we should take your column in a whole new direction."

I just looked at her blankly.

"I'm talking about giving our readers what they really want," Dana said. "Romance!"

"Oh," I said. "Sure."

"I mean, that's what a gossip column is all about, right?" Dana went on. "Who's going out with who, who has a secret crush – you know, juicy stuff."

Now that I thought about it, I realised that Dana was one hundred percent correct.

The problem is, no one's telling me any big secrets these days. Especially in the romance department.

What am I going to do now?

Dear Diary,

I was at my computer writing to Max, trying to cheer him up about the last Basher defeat, when Ashley suddenly burst in without knocking.

"Guess what?" she cried. "I've got the most amazing news!"

I sat up. I could really use some good news. Had Coach Salvatore posted an early Mighty Oaks roster somewhere? With me on it?

"Dana just called Kristin – we're all going to Harrington on Saturday! They've invited the whole school over for an afternoon social!"

"What's a social?" I asked.

"It's, um, a fun afternoon with games and stuff," Ashley said.

If you ask me, I don't think my sister has a clue

what a social is. I sure don't.

Campbell groaned. "Do we have to go?" she asked.

"I've got to practise extra hard on Saturday," I said. "Coach Salvatore's announcing final cuts after practice on Monday."

Ashley threw up her hands. "Come on, guys," she said. "We'll have a blast. And Mary-Kate, just think," she added in a lower voice. "This is your big chance with Grant."

"Who?" Campbell asked, pricking up her ears from across the room. "Hey, MK, was he that guy you were hanging out with at the Sadie Hawkins dance? He's Harrington's starting pitcher."

"He is?" I squeaked. Not only is he cute – but he's also a sports star?

I was beginning to get excited.

"You *are* going to go, aren't you, Mary-Kate?" Ashley asked anxiously.

"Sure," I said. "It sounds great."

The words were hardly out of my mouth when Ashley suddenly got this funny look on her face. It was as if she'd just thought of something really amazing.

"Sorry, guys, gotta go," she told me and Campbell. Then she bolted out of our room so fast she tore a corner off Campbell's Mia Hamm poster.

Why does Ashley keep running off like that?

chapter 10

Monday

Dear Diary,

Just a quick update while I'm downstairs in the laundry room, waiting for the dryer to finish. Mary-Kate spilled base solution all over my white blouse in lab today when Grant said hi to her. I know she's in love, Diary. She just doesn't want to admit it.

That's why I did what I'm about to tell you about.

The news about our trip to Harrington must have inspired me or something. Because right there in Mary-Kate's room, I had a stroke of total genius.

I had the most perfect story idea ever for my new-direction gossip column!

It was Mary-Kate who made me think of it. I can tell she's really dying to see Grant, no matter what she says about softball practice.

And Dana wants romance stuff for the next article, right? With secret crushes and really spicy scoops?

No problem.

I wrote a whole story on Mary-Kate and her secret crush on Grant Marino. If I do say so, it's my best work so far. Here's how I did it:

First I wrote up some basic info about Grant and Mary-Kate and how they like each other. But they haven't actually gone out or anything yet, so I couldn't add much there. I had to find a new, more interesting angle . . .

I stopped typing and frowned. What's really interesting about Mary-Kate? I wondered. In the romance department, I mean. I was pretty sure she'd only kissed one guy in her whole life.

"Kissing . . ." I mused aloud. "Hmmm . . ."

Wait! I was having a major brainstorm here!

Mary-Kate practises kissing on her pillow.

No, her arm.

The mirror?

Okay, all three! Why not?

And she pretends she's kissing Grant Marino! Perfect!

Then I stopped typing again. Could I actually say

all of this crazy stuff? I mean, Mary-Kate doesn't really practise kissing anybody on anything.

Not that I know of, anyway.

Mary-Kate won't mind' if I stretch the truth a teensy bit, right? Sisters understand things like that. Besides, gossip columns are supposed to be fun. And it isn't the same as the Lexy situation at all.

Mary-Kate has a terrific sense of humour. She'll know I'm not really being serious or anything.

As soon as I'd finished, I e-mailed the story to Dana. I was extra proud of myself for turning it in early, too. I'm absolutely positive that article is *exactly* what Dana is looking for.

And being able to do something really nice for Mary-Kate and Grant is an added bonus! All the two of them need is a little nudge in the right direction.

Just call me Cupid, Diary!

Dear Diary,

I sure hope Campbell never reads this. (If you are, Campbell, get LOST!!!) But I'm getting really excited about seeing Grant again on Saturday. Even if it does interfere with my new training programme.

It was pretty embarrassing when I spilled that base stuff on Ashley in lab today. But Grant just laughed and helped us clean it up. At least it wasn't acid or anything.

The way I figure it, the most important thing with Grant is to stay cool. I don't want to scare him off by seeming too interested. (I think I read that somewhere in one of Ashley's teen magazines.)

Oops! Hold the phone, Diary! Campbell is fooling with our alarm clock again . . .

Okay, Diary, I'm back. I asked Campbell what she was doing with the clock.

"I'm setting our alarm extra early for tomorrow morning," Campbell explained. "You know, so we can get in some pre-breakfast batting practice after our run. We can skip the weights just this once if you want."

"Gee, thanks," I said weakly. Campbell's superpacked training schedule is totally wearing me out.

But I know she's right.

If I want a spot on the Mighty Oaks, the key word is F-O-C-U-S.

Dear Diary,

Help, it's me again! It's two A.M. and I haven't been able to sleep at all. I've been tossing and turning for hours.

I keep thinking about Miss Viola and Lexy Martin. And you know what? The truth is, I can't be absolutely positive Mary-Kate will think that kissing story is funny.

I have this awful feeling that this time I've gone too far. And to make things worse, Dana has my article on her computer, ready to print!

I just can't take any chances. There's only one thing to do. I have to write a whole new article and explain the situation to Dana.

I have no choice. The way I figure it, either I face Dana now – or Mary-Kate later . . .

(3:00) Hi Diary, I'm back! And I'm feeling much better, thank you very much.

Rewriting my article wasn't as hard as I thought. (I just finished!) I made the whole thing anonymous. You know, with initials and stuff like that – "MB" likes "GM" – you get the idea. And I took out the whole kissing part.

Then I e-mailed the new story to Dana and told her to erase the old one. Yep, it was pretty embarrassing. But it would be a lot worse to risk embarrassing my own sister. Even hanging out with Dana and her whole White Oak cool crowd isn't worth *that*.

Whew! Now maybe I can get some zzzzs.

Nighty-night!

chapter 11

Saturday

Dear Diary,

Well, today was Saturday. The Big Day.
It was big, all right.

I guess I'll have to start at the
beginning. Just to warn you, Diary, it's
a long story. But don't worry, I have
plenty of time to write. I'm not leaving
my room before next week or so.

It was a long bus ride to Harrington this
morning, even though the school is just
down the road. I saved a seat for
Ashley. But get this, Diary: she
walked right past me!

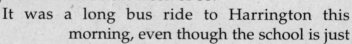

I turned around. It didn't take a
rocket scientist to figure out that
Ashley wanted to sit with Dana. She
ended up behind her, actually, with Fiona Ferris. But
that was bad enough.

Ashley kind of shrugged her shoulders at me apologetically. "I'll sit with you on the way back, okay?" she said.

I guess she thinks I'll understand because I'm her sister.

But I don't.

I felt better when Phoebe sat down with me. I really like her a lot. She's always talking about cool books and movies and all the places she's travelled with her parents. She's even been to the rain forest!

That made me think of Dad. When I woke up this morning, there was an e-mail from him on my computer. But it isn't the same as having him around all the time.

As soon as we got to Harrington, some of the guys gave us a quick mini-tour of the school. Harrington is a pretty cool place. It looks a lot like our school, actually, with its big, ivy-covered buildings and great athletic facilities.

I didn't see any gargoyles like we have all over White Oak, though. Just two stone lions outside the main gates. "They're a gift from some wealthy graduate in the early nineteen hundreds," this blond guy named Lewis told us.

"Isn't he cute?" Ashley whispered to me.

I nodded. But I didn't think Lewis was half as

cute as Grant. Where was Grant, anyway? Maybe I wasn't even going to get to see him. Bummer.

After the tour we all split up. Ashley headed straight for the game room to find Ross.

I started to follow her, but I didn't want to be a third wheel. So I stopped to check out the Harrington trophy cases.

They're pretty impressive, I have to admit. The cases reach all the way from the floor to the ceiling, and they take up an entire wall. I wonder how many trophies the Mighty Oaks have won.

So guess who came up as I was standing there? Grant Marino!

"Hey, Mary-Kate, what's up?" he asked.

"Not much," I said. I couldn't help staring at Grant's gorgeous dark eyes.

We talked for a while, mostly about the trophies. Then I noticed that Grant was carrying a mitt.

"I'm on my way to a pickup game," he said. "You're into softball, right? Do you want to play?"

He had to be kidding! "Does Sammy Sosa like to hit?" I answered eagerly.

"Great," Grant said. He smiled at me, and my legs got all wobbly. "Do you mind if we stop by the game room first? I need to let some of the guys know the field's been changed."

"No problem," I said. "I'll go anywhere with you."

Grant looked confused.

My face instantly went hot. *Oh, no*! Did I really say that? Out *loud*?

"I mean, let's go." I tried to cover quickly. "Anywhere. To play ball."

So much for playing it cool!

Whoops, I'll have to catch you later, Diary. I need to turn out the lights right now. Ashley's pounding on my door and I'm pretending not to be here. More on that later. Let me just say – she is no longer my sister.

Dear Diary,

Well, I tried to talk to Mary-Kate again a little while ago. But I think she was hiding from me.

It's after lights-out now, and I'm writing this in the bathroom. That way no one will hear me if I start crying.

Today was so awful that I'm not sure I can write anything at all. But maybe it will make me feel better if I do . . .

So here goes: Ross and I were supposed to meet in the game room at Harrington this morning. But when I got there, I didn't see him anywhere.

That's funny, I thought. No one was playing Ping-Pong or video games, either.

Then I spotted a whole bunch of guys hanging out on one side of the room. They were all gathered around – who else? – Dana Woletsky.

And Ross was there, too!

No one even noticed me as I walked over. That's because they were all completely focused on Dana.

And whatever she was reading aloud.

I edged closer so I could hear what she was saying.

"'Have you heard about the couple who met at the Sadie Hawkins Dance last month?'" Dana read.

I just stood there, frozen to the spot. I recognised those words – they were mine!

Dana was reading from my gossip column. And she wasn't reading the version I told her to print. She was reading the *first* version!

"'They're crazy about each other but haven't had a date yet,'" Dana went on. "'Need a few hints? 1. They're both amazing ball players (one's in a bit of a slump right now – wonder why?) 2. They're both huge Chicago Cubs fans. 3. They're both newbies at White Oak and Harrington. This week's Cupid Couple is: Mary-Kate Burke and Grant Marino!'"

I felt so ill, I couldn't move. I finally ran over just as the guys started cracking up. Dana was getting to the Mary-Kate-practising-her-kissing part!

"She's in loooooove!" a guy hooted.

What should I do? I thought wildly.

Now all the boys were making gross kissing sounds and laughing even harder.

Suddenly, I heard a gasp behind me. I spun around.

It was Mary-Kate! And Grant was right behind her. The poor guy looked totally confused.

All the boys went crazy then, laughing and joking and teasing. Mary-Kate just stood there for a moment with her mouth hanging open.

Then she turned practically purple and ran out of the room.

What have I done?

Dana gave me a mean, satisfied smile. "Hey, guys, " she told everyone in the room. "Meet our star White Oak snoop: Ashley Burke. And guess what? She's Mary-Kate's sister. Her *twin* sister."

"Dana, how could you?" I cried.

Ross was looking at me all funny. But I didn't care. I didn't have time to try to explain anything now.

I had to find Mary-Kate – fast!

Dear Diary,

Okay, the coast is clear – I'm back! Ashley's gone and Campbell's snoring away. I'm trying to write by her purple lava lamp. I think it's making my page wavy.

Sorry, Diary, but I just can't tell you what happened in the Harrington game room. It's too horrible to even think about. Let's just say that Grant Marino will probably never smile at me again.

How could Ashley put all that crazy stuff in her column? I mean, me kissing a *mirror*? That's not even true!

And how am I ever going to face Grant Marino? Not to mention every single person at White Oak and Harrington.

At least there's one thing I won't have to worry about any more. Grant will never ask me out now. Hey, who could blame him?

I am never, *ever* going to speak to Ashley again.

After everything happened that I'm not writing about, I was so freaked that I ran out of the game room. I heard Ashley calling me, but I didn't stop. I just had to get out of there.

Once I was outside, I didn't know where to go or what to do. I thought about running back to one of the White Oak buses and hiding there. But we weren't leaving Harrington until after dinner. That was a long time to wait.

Then I heard the sound of cheers rising up from one of the ball fields down the hill.

The game! I remembered suddenly. Then I stopped myself.

No way, I thought. I can't go down there now. Everyone will laugh their heads off at me and Grant.

I looked over my shoulder at the White Oak buses. Then I turned back toward the cheering sounds. Which way should I go?

Actually, the answer was pretty clear. Like I said before, I'm no quitter.

Get it together, Mary-Kate, I told myself. I took a deep breath. Only one thing Ashley wrote about in that column was true: I have a major crush on Grant Marino.

Big deal. Lots of people have crushes. They just don't want to admit it. So what if everyone laughed?

At least I could show the whole world that Mary-Kate had guts.

It was time to play ball!

You know what, Diary? I really want to finish this, but I'm so tired I can hardly move my pen. I'm also starving. Maybe I'll try and sneak down to the vending machines while everyone's asleep. That way, I won't have to face anyone.

I'll write more tomorrow, okay?

Dear Diary,

Sorry about the interruption. Two girls came into the bathroom. And of course they were talking about Mary-Kate and Grant.

I thought they would never leave. So where was I, Diary?

I looked all over Harrington for Mary-Kate after she ran away. But I couldn't find her.

I knew my sister was upset. *Really* upset. I was furious with Dana – but I was even madder at myself.

Okay, so Dana double-crossed me and printed the article I told her not to print. I just know she did it on purpose, too. Mary-Kate was right: Dana isn't a very nice person.

But I never should have written the article to begin with. I guess I've been pretty selfish lately. I've been all caught up in trying to be a star and getting in with Dana. But becoming superpopular sure isn't worth losing my best friend!

Double cross

I really needed to tell Mary-Kate that it was all a big mistake. And how sorry I was!

I finally found her at the ball field. I probably should have looked there first. I guess I figured she'd be hiding somewhere. But Mary-Kate's pretty tough.

Anyway, when I got to the field, Mary-Kate's side was batting.

"Mary-Kate!" I called, running up to the fence behind the dugout. "It's me, Ashley. Over here!"

Mary-Kate was holding two bats and taking practice swings at an imaginary ball. Campbell went over to her and pointed in my direction, but Mary-Kate didn't turn around.

"Hey, Mary-Kate!" I shouted again.

"Batter up!" someone called, at almost the same time.

Mary-Kate let go of one of the bats and let it fall to the ground. Then she headed towards the plate.

"Good luck, Mary-Kate!" I cheered. But she pretended not to hear me.

I felt like that bat she'd dropped on the ground.

Serves me right.

chapter 12

Sunday

Dear Diary,

It's a miracle! Campbell actually let me
skip our early morning workout.
She shut off the alarm so I could
sleep in.

Maybe she felt sorry for me about
the whole Buzz thing. Or maybe she
just knows how tired I am after the
game yesterday.

As I came up to the plate for my first at bat of the
White Oak-Harrington game, I adjusted my helmet
and took a few last practice swings. I could hear
Ashley calling to me from behind the dugout, but I
ignored her.

Focus, I reminded myself.
I forgot about Ashley.
I forgot about Grant.
I pushed all the rotten

luck I'd been having lately on the ball field out of my mind. Pretend you're back home in Chicago, playing with the Bashers, I told myself.

"Knock one home, MK!" Campbell called.

The pitcher – a guy from Harrington – went into his wind-up.

And just then, I heard the shortstop make some stupid kissy-kissy noise.

Boy, did that steam me up.

Crack! I had a hit!

I started to run. The crowd cheered me on – and I made it to second! I hadn't heard so much cheering for a long time. It was a pretty cool feeling.

Things got better and better.

In the next inning I made an important save at first. "Way to go, MK!" Campbell said, slapping me on the back.

I made a triple play in the next inning. Charlotte Atherton jogged up to me. "What *did* you have for breakfast?" she asked.

I exchanged a grin with Campbell. "Carbs," I answered.

By the time the bottom of the ninth rolled around, I was having a great time. The magic was back!

It was a close call, but our team won, eight to six.

And I didn't hear any more kissy noises!

But that wasn't all. I almost fell over when Coach Salvatore came up to me after the game! She'd been in the crowd the whole time.

"Mary-Kate, I think we can safely say you've proved yourself," she told me. "Congratulations. Consider yourself an official member of the Mighty Oaks!"

I couldn't believe it. The day turned out to be pretty amazing after all.

But let's make one thing perfectly clear. My ex-sister is *not* off the hook!

Dear Diary,

In case you were wondering what happened to me last night, Miss Viola kicked me out of the bathroom and personally escorted me back to Room 25.

So anyway, after the softball game, there was a big barbecue down by the Harrington field house. Ross found me at the game (I wasn't hard to miss, screaming for Mary-Kate!) and the two of us went together.

He didn't say very much at first.

"I know what you're probably thinking," I said finally. "That was a pretty rotten thing I did to Mary-Kate and Grant."

Ross just kind of shrugged and looked at the ground.

"I really really didn't mean for things to turn out this way," I tried to explain. Then I told him the whole story.

Luckily, Ross was pretty understanding. He shook his head as he heaped my plate with ribs, chili and dinner rolls. "I've known Dana since we were little kids," he said. "She can be mean sometimes."

He spooned up a huge portion of potato salad for himself. "I'm sure you'll fix things with Mary-Kate," he added. "I have a younger brother at home, and we fight all the time. But we always get over it."

"I sure hope so," I said with a sigh. Mary-Kate and I had had big fights before. But somehow I had a feeling this was different.

I looked over my shoulder at Mary-Kate. She was sitting with a whole bunch of players from the game. She seemed to be having a good time. But every time I tried to catch her eye, she looked away.

Dana was holding court at a table crowded with Harrington jocks. She and her friends laughed at every single thing the guys said. Typical.

It's a no-brainer that I'll never have anything to do with Dana again. I don't care how popular she is.

Grant only showed up for about two seconds.

He grabbed a bunch of food, then disappeared somewhere. Probably back to his dorm.

I gazed down at my own plate of barbecue. It's a good thing Ross had a really good appetite. Because right then I didn't feel like eating one bite.

I really wanted to help Mary-Kate and Grant get together, Diary. I just went about it the wrong way. Totally wrong.

It sure was a long day. When we finally got back to White Oak, everyone hung around downstairs in the Porter House lounge until lights-out. They were all talking about the fantastic time they had at Harrington.

I went straight upstairs to my room. I needed to be by myself for a while.

Because it's official, Diary. Mary-Kate is definitely not speaking to me. She even got on the other bus to go home.

So I have only one thing on my mind.

How can I make things up to Mary-Kate?

chapter 13

Monday

Dear Diary,

By now the whole world must know about my crush on Grant Marino. It's been a big topic of conversation here at White Oak for the last two days.

But hey – I can deal with it. I have to.

Ashley wrote me a note and slipped it under my door, but I tore it up without reading it. I didn't return any of her e-mails, either. And I've been sitting with Phoebe instead of Ashley in the dining hall.

"Honest, I had nothing to do with it, Mary-Kate," Phoebe said at dinner last night. "I had no idea—"

"No problem, Phoebe," I broke in. "It's not your fault. This is between Ashley and me."

Then I helped Phoebe practise her lines for her *Romeo and Juliet* audition. This drama stuff actually seems kind of cool. And if there's anyone who understands about try-outs, it's me!

By the way, I saw Grant in lab today, but this time he didn't even say hi. He turned bright red when I walked past his table, too. So it's totally over with Grant, before it even started.

I've been e-mailing Max a lot, trying to help him come up with ways to save the Bashers. Those guys are really in trouble now. They're five-zip so far.

So between softball practice and schoolwork and writing to Dad and Carrie and Max and helping Phoebe with her lines, I'm keeping pretty busy.

But hey, I still have time to be mad at Ashley.

Dear Diary,

Well, I've tried everything, but Mary-Kate won't even let me explain. My only chance is Phoebe. But first I have to convince her to stop being mad at me herself. And then maybe she'll talk to Mary-Kate.

It took a lot of explaining this afternoon, but in the end Phoebe came around.

"Well, I've never trusted Dana," she said. "I can see her switching the articles on purpose. But Ashley, why did you write those stories about Mary-Kate in the first place?"

I sighed and looked down at the swirly pattern in

my duvet. "I wish I knew," I said. "I just got carried away, I guess. I was trying to give Mary-Kate and Grant a little push."

Phoebe raised her eyebrows.

"But mostly I was trying to impress everyone with a funny column," I finished in a small voice. "I thought Mary-Kate would understand that."

"I'm not sure I can convince Mary-Kate to forgive you," Phoebe said. "She's really upset."

"Well, I have an idea," I told my roommate. "I'm going to write an apology to Mary-Kate in my next column. I'll tell everyone that I made all that stuff up."

Phoebe nodded. "Sounds like a plan."

"And then I'm giving up that stupid gossip column for good," I said. "Even if it means I won't get to work on the *Acorn* any more."

Phoebe thought for a minute. "Wait," she said. "Now I have an idea. Ashley, you've got a great sense of style. A lot different from mine, but still . . . Why don't you ask Ms. Bloomberg if you could write a different kind of column? You know, like 'Fashion Tips from Ashley' or something."

"Phoebe, you're brilliant!" I cried. I was so excited I jumped straight off my bed. "How about 'Fashion Tips from Ashley and Phoebe'? We could write it together – and cover everything from super-trendy to vintage!"

Phoebe gave me a big grin. "Sounds like a winning idea to me," she said. "So we're partners?"

"You bet!" I said, giving my roomie a high five.

Now all I have to do is talk to Mary-Kate.

Hey, Diary,

Yep, it's me again! And you won't believe what's happened.

Here goes . . .

Tonight after dinner I had it out with Ashley. I went up to her room to see Phoebe, but Phoebe wasn't there. I think I was set up.

Ashley told me what happened – that she'd decided to pull one article and substitute another, but Dana had double-crossed her.

That explained a lot of things, I guess. But I was still upset. And Ashley just didn't seem to understand why.

"Mary-Kate, I told Dana not to print that article," Ashley said. "It's not my fault the wrong one got into the paper."

"You shouldn't have written either of them in the first place," I pointed out. "I'm supposed to be able to trust you with anything, Ashley. Even my deepest, darkest secrets."

"But you can," Ashley insisted.

"Ha!" I snorted. "Those weren't even secrets you wrote about. They were total lies."

Ashley couldn't argue with that.

"I can't believe my own sister would make up something really embarrassing about me – and print it for the whole world to read!" I went on, pacing around the room. "How can I ever trust you again?"

"Can't you just forgive and forget?" Ashley said. "Please, Mary-Kate? I promise, I'll never, ever do anything like that again."

I shook my head. "I really want to forgive you, Ashley. But I just can't right now. Something's changed between us, I guess."

"Nothing's changed!" Ashley insisted. "I'm still your best friend. You *have* to forgive me."

I was about to answer her. But then, Diary, the most amazing thing happened!

Miss Viola came running up the stairs and told us we had a phone call – from our dad!

Ashley and I looked at each other in surprise. Dad had only called us from the Amazon once before. Was this some kind of emergency? Had something terrible happened?

The two of us rushed downstairs to the phone. We held the receiver between us so we could both talk to Dad at once.

"It's so great to hear your voice!" Ashley said.

"Are you calling from the middle of the jungle?" I asked.

Dad laughed. "Actually, I'm calling from *Chicago*."

Dad, where are you?

Chicago? I almost dropped my part of the phone. Ashley's mouth was hanging open.

"Well, Carrie and I missed you two so much that we worked extra hard and finished up our project early," Dad said. "So we're already home."

I started jumping up and down. "All right!" I shouted in Ashley's ear. "When can we see you?"

"Very soon," our dad replied. "How does Wednesday night sound?"

"It sounds great!" I told him. I hadn't felt so happy in ages. "I can't wait to see you!"

"Me neither, Dad," Ashley said.

After we'd said goodbye and hung up, Ashley and I stood there for a minute, still in shock. Then we grabbed each other and started dancing down the hall together.

Until I remembered how mad I still was at Ashley.

There's just one problem, Diary. The two of us can't let our big fight spoil Dad's visit.

So I guess Ashley and I *have* to make up by Wednesday.

chapter 14

Wednesday

Dear Diary,

It was so fantastic to find Dad waiting for me and Mary-Kate in the main foyer tonight.

"You look really handsome, Dad," I told him as he gave us both a huge hug.

Dad did look great. He was wearing his navy blazer and grey trousers. He was super tanned, too.

"And you girls are as beautiful as ever," Dad said. "I guess White Oak life really agrees with you."

"It sure does," I said. Mary-Kate just nodded.

Dad took us to a cosy Italian restaurant. I was glad I'd got all dressed up in my flowered skirt and slingback heels. Mary-Kate was wearing her favourite black cords and a black turtleneck sweater.

The waiters were so nice to us. I guess they could

tell it was a special occasion. We ordered lasagna and garlic bread and a huge pizza. Dad wanted everything on it – I guess they don't have pepperoni and hot sausage in the Amazon!

Anyway, we told Dad about all the things we've been doing at White Oak. Then he told us about his and Carrie's big adventures in the rain forest. Once they saw a panther sleeping in a tree. And once Carrie almost sat in a nest of fire ants. A few of them crawled up her trouser leg.

Ouch!

It sounded like such a cool place. I'd really like to go there some time.

Dad brought us presents, too: a real dart gun for Mary-Kate and a beaded mask for me. Double cool!

"So, girls, I'm going to try and come up to White Oak every weekend to visit for the rest of the term," Dad said. "Mary-Kate, I won't miss a single Mighty Oaks softball game. And Ashley, maybe we could take some of your friends from White Oak and Harrington out bowling some time."

"Perfect!" I said, totally psyched.

But Mary-Kate frowned. "But Dad, you're home now," she said. "We don't have to stay here at White Oak any more. Aren't you going to take us back to Chicago with you?"

Dad looked surprised. "Well, sure, Mary-Kate. I guess you can come home if you want. But it sounds like you're having such a good time at White Oak. And you just made the softball team. Are you sure that's what you want to do?"

Mary-Kate didn't answer right away. Then she took a deep breath. "Yes, Dad," she said.

I couldn't believe what I'd just heard. Mary-Kate would rather go home with Dad than stay here at White Oak with me!

Then she went on. "The Bashers want me back. And I want to go."

She didn't even look at me after she said it. She just kept twisting the corner of the red-checked tablecloth.

I was so shocked I couldn't say anything at all. And I was hurt, too. Mary-Kate chose the Bashers over me!

Dad looked pretty stunned, too. "Ashley," he said, "do you want to come home?"

I thought about it for a minute. Sure, I missed Dad and Carrie and our friends back in Chicago. But then I remembered all my new friends at White Oak (I didn't count Dana), my new column with Phoebe at the paper, and the zillions of cute boys over at Harrington. Especially Ross.

But what about my sister?

Maybe Mary-Kate's right, I thought. Maybe

things have changed between us. She's made it pretty clear that she's willing to separate, right? So I guess I'm willing, too.

"No, Dad," I said slowly. "I want to stay."

Dear Diary,

I thought Dad was going to fall straight into his spaghetti tonight when Ashley and I told him we wanted to split up. I mean, the two of us have never really been apart in our whole lives.

After Ashley said she was going to stay at White Oak, I just stared at her. "You can't do that, Ashley," I said, frowning. "You have to come back to Chicago. That's where we live, remember?"

Ashley bit her lip. "I'm sorry, Mary-Kate. I'll really, really miss you if you go home. But it's only until the end of the school year. I'm just not ready to leave White Oak yet."

Dad looked at both of us. "Girls, this is a pretty major decision. Don't you want to, uh, think about it for a little while?"

"NO!" Ashley and I both said at once.

Dad put down his napkin. "Well, I guess we have

a stalemate," he said. "Why don't you both sleep on this and we'll talk again in the morning?"

"Okay, Dad," Ashley said. "That's fair, I guess."

"Fine with me," I said.

But I'm not going to change my mind, Diary.

chapter 15

Thursday

Dear Diary,

Well, Ashley and I gave Dad our decisions at breakfast this morning.

I told you I wasn't going to change my mind.

Well, Ashley didn't change hers, either.

So here I am, packing up my trunk to go home with Dad. Campbell's at the gym, working out. I think she's a little upset. She's coming back in time to say goodbye, though.

"But MK, you can't just leave!" Campbell said, when I gave her the news. "The Oaks need you!"

No, I thought. The Bashers need me. We just have to make it to the championships this season. The Oaks already have plenty of great players. Like Campbell.

I'm going to miss Campbell, too. But I'll miss Ashley even more. But it's only for a couple of months. Maybe it will be good for us, especially after everything that's happened lately. I'm not even mad at Ashley any more. Honest.

And hey, I'll keep writing in this diary. Maybe I'll even let Ashley read *mine* for a change!

Whoops, I think Dad's knocking on the door. See ya, Diary!

Dear Diary,

So this is it. Mary-Kate is actually leaving!

Last night, after Dad dropped the two of us back at White Oak, we each went up to our own rooms without speaking to each other.

We weren't angry or anything. Just stunned.

I'm going down to Mary-Kate's room in a minute to help her pack. It's going to be hard, Diary. The two of us are going to be on our own for the first time ever!

But hey, Mary-Kate and I are making our own decisions here, living our own lives. Everyone – even twins – has to do that sooner or later.

Right?

We've already promised to e-mail each other every day. We'll probably call a lot, too. That way, I can find out about everything that's going on back home and Mary-Kate can hear all the news from White Oak. We're both going to be super busy, so the term will be over before we know it.

But I can't help wondering, Diary. Will things ever be the same between me and Mary-Kate again?

White Oak
Academy

Wish you were here...

Wish you were here!

P.S. Wish You Were Here

Dear Diary,
I'm so mad, I can barely write. My hand is even shaking. You won't believe this – but I found out where my lost book report is.

My cousin Jeremy took it. He stole it on purpose. And he turned it in for his English class with *his* name on it!

The worst thing is, he refuses to do anything about it.

"You've got to go back to your English teacher, right now," I said when I found out what happened. "And get the book report back."

"No way," Jeremy replied. "Just chill, Ashley.

"No one's going to find out about this. We won't get caught. And I'll never do it again, okay?"

"I don't believe this!" I cried. "Jeremy, this is plagiarism!"

But he wouldn't listen. And now I don't know what to do. If he gets caught, I'm going to be in deep trouble, too.

I have got to talk to Mary-Kate about this. But she's back in Chicago – and I'm here at White Oak. I keep e-mailing her – and she's not writing back!

This afternoon I wanted to talk to her so badly I left lunch early and sneaked back to Porter House. I dialled home and crossed my fingers. But Mary-Kate wasn't there. I didn't even leave a message. It's too humiliating. I'm not going to beg her to call me if she won't even answer my e-mails.

So now I'm totally upset. My sister hates me. My cousin's a rat. How did I get into this mess? And how am I going to get out of it?

I wish Mary-Kate were here!

Dear Diary,

First of all, I'm not going to mention Ashley. But she still hasn't called me, written me, or even sent me an e-mail! And it's been two weeks!

Now on to my real problems.

For the past two days, I've been cutting softball

102

practise to go to play rehearsals – and lying about it to everyone. I feel really guilty about it, too.

On Wednesday, I told Amanda I had a dentist appointment after school so I wouldn't have to go to softball practice. I even pretended to walk home, then sneaked back to the theatre just in time to go on stage.

Thursday, I ran into Brian and Max right after school. "See you at practice," they said.

"Oh, gosh, " I said, trying to sound sick. "I think I'm getting the flu. I might not make it."

"Mary-Kate, what did you come home from boarding school for, if you're not going to play softball?" Max asked me.

That's a good question. I really want to help the Belmont Bashers win the championship. But I like acting in *Peter Pan* so much, I don't want to give that up, either.

I don't know what to do! And the only person I can ask is halfway across the country.

Why hasn't Ashley called me even once? Doesn't she know that I need her sometimes? Like now. I could really use her advice.

But to tell you the truth, I'm so mad at her right now, I don't think I'd speak to her if she did call!

mary-kateandashley

TWO of a kind ™

Rs 99/- each

Coming soon – can you collect them all?

HarperCollins *Children's Books*

mary-kateandashley

TWO of a kind™

Rs 99/- each

Coming soon – can you collect them all?

HarperCollins *Children's Books*

mary-kate and ashley TWO of a kind ™

Rs 99/- each

Coming soon – can you collect them all?

Come discover friends.....

HarperCollins *Children's Books*